First published in Great Britain in 2003 by Frances Lincoln Limited,

4 Torriano Mews, Torriano Avenue, London NW5 2RZ

www.franceslincoln.com

British Library Cataloguing in Publication Data available on request

ISBN 0-7112-1946-X

Set in Frutiger Condensed, Footlight and Fontesque

Printed in China

1 3 5 7 9 10 8 6 4 2

THE Fairy-Spotter's Handbook

Rosalind Kerven

Illustrated by
Wayne Anderson

FRANCES LINCOLN

For Jennifer and Natasha ~ R.K.
For Lauren and Millie Rose ~ W.A.

Contents

Do You Believe in Fairies?

Have you ever heard a rustling in the shadows, strange echoes of laughter – and then caught a glimpse of something small flitting away? Not a mouse, not a creepy crawly… but some other creature, wild – yet almost human.

Is it male or female? It could be either. Grown-up or child? It's hard to tell. It might be green like leaves – green skin, green hair, green clothes, swaying and dancing outside with the wind. Or it might be faded like moths, brown, grey or pale as the moon.

You think you see it – but then, in the blink of an eye, it disappears!

Could it be a fairy?

Sshh! Don't say that name aloud! It's best to call them the Good Folk or the Little People, the Cipenapers or the Fanes, the Hookeys, the Elves, the Sprites or the Gentry.

Whatever name you choose, don't say anything to upset them. It doesn't take much to turn the fairies against you, and they'll seize any chance to tease you with their mischievous tricks.

But do something to please them, and they'll shower you with wishes and gifts, do little jobs for you and help you out of trouble.

Can all this be true? Are fairies real? Listen to the folklore and old people's stories from round the fireside long, long ago…

Dancing Fairies

At midnight or on May Day, at full moon
or Hallowe'en, you have a good chance
of seeing some dancing fairies!
They'll be out in the loneliest part of the countryside,
under the hills, beneath gnarled, twisted trees, beside
ancient ruined castles. As the sun sets and the light
fades, there comes a distant sound of music –
an eerie, heart-stopping rhythm of harp, pipe,
fiddle and drum. It grows louder, wilder as
the moon comes up…

And then, rising from the ground like
a mist, come the pale fairy dancers.
They're a whirlwind of spinning,
shrieking laughter. They're leaping,
twirling, dipping, tapping; they're
endlessly, endlessly moving.

They dance all night. But as soon as the
first streaks of dawn light the morning
sky, suddenly they stop. They put
on their caps, wrap themselves
in billowing cloaks.
And then – they vanish!

The Man who
Spied on the Fairies

An old fellow went up the hill one night to spy on the fairies. He planned to catch the fairy king and queen inside his hat. His eyes almost popped out of his head when he saw them dancing – because not one of them was bigger than his thumbnail!

But the fairies are no fools, and they guessed what he was up to. They put a spell on him so that he couldn't move. They pricked him all over with their tiny swords, and danced on top of his nose. Then they tied him up in a net made of cobwebs and rolled him right down again to the bottom of the hill!

Fairyland

Fairies come from Fairyland, a secret country that lies deep under the ground.
Some people call it 'the Hidden Country' or 'the Twilight Realm' for the sun
never shines there and no moon or stars light the sky. It's a beautiful, rolling
land of rivers, woods and flowers. There are golden palaces, farms with fat
milk cows, and orchards full of huge, juicy fruits. Everything is perfect.
Time stands still and the days go on forever. The fairies never grow old or ill,
nor do they ever die. All day long they play music, dance
and hold wonderful, mouth-watering feasts.

Fairy horses have silver shoes
and bells in their manes.

Fairy dogs are white
with red ears.

Fairies fly by saying a magic word, wearing
a magic cap or riding a horse or a bundle of stalks.

Can you find your way into Fairyland?

A long tunnel through a thicket of thorns could lead to Fairyland.

This big stone on a hill
could be a door
into Fairyland.

Sometimes people get lost in a mist,

and when it clears away, they find themselves in Fairyland.

But beware! A visit to Fairyland might change you for ever…

People who claim they have been to Fairyland often seem strange when they come back.
They might be lame from hours of crazy dancing. They might become very quiet and serious.
They might have strange dreams. They might wander off to lonely places, always searching
for a way back to the secret kingdom of Fairyland.

The Golden Ball

Elidor was a real person who lived in Wales about 800 years ago. He claimed that when he was twelve years old, he ran away from school and hid in a forest, and there he met two fairy men. They led him down a secret tunnel to Fairyland, and took him to the fairy king. The king commanded him to play with his son, a young fairy prince.

At first Elidor had a wonderful time, but after a while he grew homesick. He stole a golden ball from the fairy prince and ran back through the tunnel to show it to his mother.

But he had been seen! Two fairy men followed him and seized the golden ball from his hand.

After that, Elidor never found the way into Fairyland again.

The Secret Door

Two musicians were out walking one snowy night, when they met a strange little old man. "Come this way," he said. "We need some music for our party."

He led them out to a lonely place in the hills. There he stamped on the ground – and at once a secret door opened. The musicians followed him through it. They found themselves in a brilliantly-lit room overflowing with fairies! The musicians took up their fiddles and played a tune. At once, all the fairies began dancing.

The dance went on for hours and hours. When it ended, the little old man led the musicians out to the hill again. He gave them each a bag of gold – and vanished.

The two musicians hurried home. When they arrived, they were astonished to find that all the people and buildings looked completely different. For while it seemed to them that they had spent just one night in Fairyland, a hundred years had passed in the real world outside!

Fairy Queens and Kings

In Fairyland there are many different kingdoms, and each one is ruled by a Fairy queen or king. These queens and kings are astonishingly beautiful, but their hearts are as cold as moon-dazzled ice, and strange enchantments flow from their finger-tips.

★ They can change their shapes, and turn themselves into animals or monsters!

★ Sometimes they capture people and keep them imprisoned as slaves!

★ They can conjure up weird visions and dreams!

★ They can turn people blind just by touching their eyes!

★ They can sing people to sleep for a hundred years!

The Magic Apple

A man called Thomas the Rhymer was snatched away by a fairy queen, because she wanted to listen to the beautiful music he played on his harp.

"Don't you dare to say a single word while you are in Fairyland," she warned him. "If you do, I shall keep you here for ever!"

Thomas managed to stay silent for seven whole years, and so at last the queen had to set him free. As a parting gift, she gave him a magic apple. After he had eaten it, Thomas found that he could speak nothing but the truth and he could foresee what would happen in the future.

These strange powers made him famous – but also very unhappy.

House Fairies

House fairies are magical, tiny old men who love doing household jobs – but only when no one is looking.

 Some wear raggedy clothes. Some have long, shaggy beards. Some have cross, wizened faces.

 They live in musty, dusty nooks and crannies of houses, especially old-fashioned houses in out-of-the-way places.

SERVAN — found in Italy and Switzerland.

BROWNIE — found in England and Scotland

If you notice that household chores have been done when no one is around, you almost certainly have a fairy in the house!

 House fairies are found in many different countries.

KOBOLD — found in Germany

NIS — found in Denmark and Norway

TOMTE — found in Sweden

DUENDE — found in Spain and Portugal)

Mischief and Tricks

House fairies are awkward and easily offended. They have terrible tempers and often play nasty tricks – so some people try to get rid of them. They beg the fairies to go away and leave them alone, but the fairies always refuse. Even if a family moves house to escape them, the fairies sneak after them and move into their new home.

Can you spot the six different tricks the fairies are playing in this house?

1   2   3

4   5   6

Answers ☆ 1 pulling quilts off people's beds ☆ 2 tickling people who are asleep ☆ 3 hiding things ☆ 4 making plates fall off the shelves ☆ 5 making the washing dirty ☆ 6 tripping people up

How to Spot a House Fairy

If there's an open fire in your house, you might see a house fairy running up and down the chimney instead of using the front door to go in and out.

You could ask a grown-up to light the fire, and watch it burning low after everyone has gone to bed. A fairy might come out in the middle of the night and sit by the fire to keep warm. Look out for his sooty footprints in the morning.

It's also a good idea to leave out a small bowl of food at night. Fairies love plain, simple dishes like milk and porridge. If the bowl is empty in the morning, you will know who's eaten it!

Fairy Treasure

Fairies love all kinds of treasure: money, gold, silver and shimmering precious stones. They hide it in dark, secret places.

Some fairies can actually make treasure grow from nothing! Some can turn rubbish into gold – and gold into rubbish.

Next time one of your baby teeth falls out, put it under your pillow before you go to sleep. A fairy might take it away in the night, and leave a small piece of treasure in its place.

Fool's Gold

Two men were walking through the mountains one night when they saw some fairies having a party. The fairies called them over and began to dance around them. A little old fairy man pointed to a pile of coal and told the men to take some. Then a distant clock struck midnight – and the fairies vanished.

The next morning the men found that all the coal had turned into gold!

But one of these men was greedy. He went searching for the fairies again the next night, and when he found them he stole some more of their magic coal.

What a fool! The next morning it was still coal – and the gold he already had was turned back into coal too. Even worse, the fairies punished his greed by making all his hair fall out.

Leprechauns

Leprechauns are Irish fairies who work as shoe-makers. Every leprechaun has his own secret store of treasure, which he keeps in a special crock buried in the ground.

If you ever meet a leprechaun, he'll probably be very friendly and offer to show you where his gold is hidden. But be warned: he's probably only teasing, and he'll soon play a cunning trick to make sure you never find the gold!

The Field of Thistles

A man once met a friendly leprechaun who said he would take him to the spot where his treasure was buried. They set off and came to a field full of thistles. The leprechaun stopped in the middle and said, "There, it's under that thistle."

The man grew very excited. But first he had to go home and fetch his spade to dig up the treasure. He pulled off one of his bright red socks and tied it to the thistle the leprechaun had shown him: that way, he was sure to remember where the treasure was. "Please don't take this sock away," he begged. "Oh, I won't," the little fellow promised.

The man dashed off to fetch his spade, and came back again as fast as he could. The sock was exactly where he had left it. But the leprechaun had also tied a red sock to every other thistle in the field – hundreds and hundreds of them! So the poor man never found the treasure after all.

Friendly Fairies

Some kinds of fairy are really friendly. They like to borrow clothes and tools from people and lend their own things in return.

These fairies are especially kind and helpful to people who are in trouble. They are very generous and enjoy giving wonderful magic gifts to their human friends. Of course, the most precious fairy gift of all is a wish – or maybe even three wishes.

If you are ever lucky enough to be given a gift by a fairy, take great care to use it in the right way. Otherwise you might waste it or even lose it…

A fairy once gave a man a magic sack full of delicious bread and cheese. However much he ate, the sack was always full. One day, a poor old beggar asked him to share some of the food, but the man refused – and the magic sack disappeared for ever!

The Girl who Flew with the Fairies

A girl called Anne Jeffries longed to see some fairies. One day she was sitting in her garden when six tiny men dressed in green suddenly appeared. They bowed, jumped into her lap and pricked her eyes so she couldn't see. The next minute she found herself flying through the air!

When she landed, the fairies said a magic word to make her see again. She saw that she was in a beautiful wood, with silver and gold palaces and temples dotted amongst the trees. The fairies danced and played with her for hours before they took her home.

After that, even when Anne was grown up, the fairies came to see her. They brought her little presents and gave her the magic gift of healing people who were ill.

Dangerous Fairies

Unfortunately, many fairies are sly, slippery tricksters. They appear out of nowhere and pretend to be quite friendly. But the next minute they suddenly do something nasty, or cast a horrible spell!

ELLEFOLK live in Denmark, Norway and Sweden. Their breath can make people ill. Their favourite trick is to persuade a boy to join in their wild, twirling dances. Afterwards, he will never grow any bigger for the rest of his life.

SALVANELLI are Italian fairies. If they see a traveller walking up a mountain path, they run ahead of him as if to lead the way – then vanish, leaving the poor traveller wobbling on the edge of a cliff.

DAMES VERTES ('Green Ladies') are beautiful French fairies who hide in woods. They love to lead people astray through the trees, grab them by the hair and dangle them over a waterfall.

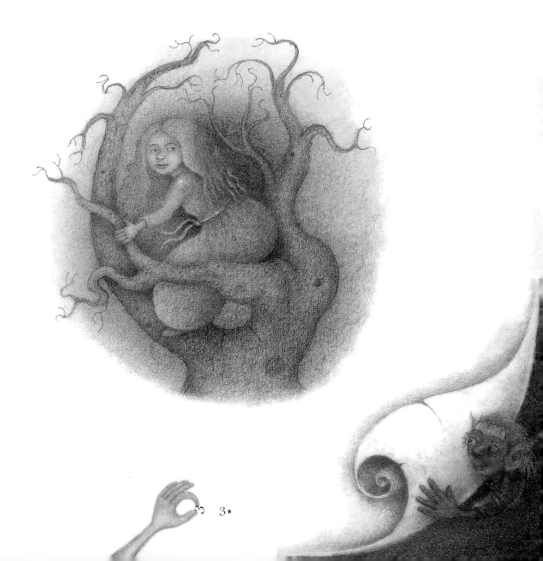

Some of the most dangerous fairies lurk in the rippling, murky depths of rivers, lakes and ponds. They lure people in if they get the chance – and drown them.

WILL O' THE WISPS live in the damp, boggy swamps and marshes of England. They shine a flickering light in front of travellers – who follow it until they fall into the water.

NIXIES are German water fairies that look like mermaids. They drag victims down to their underwater palaces.

KELPIES are Scottish fairies
in the shape of horses.
If you meet a kelpie,
it will persuade you
to jump on its back —
then plunge down into
the depths of a river!

DRACAE live in France.
They tempt people by floating
golden rings or cups in the river.
As soon as someone tries to
reach the gold, the dracae pull
him down into the water.

Protect Yourself From Dangerous Fairies

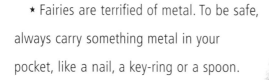

★ Fairies are terrified of metal. To be safe, always carry something metal in your pocket, like a nail, a key-ring or a spoon.

★ If you ever go into a strange house where a fairy might be lurking, stick a pin in the door to stop it magically closing behind you and trapping you inside.

★ Wear a clove of garlic round your neck: fairies can't bear the smell!

★ Put the branch of a rowan tree (mountain ash) on your window-sill or doorstep. This will frighten the fairies away.

★ If you get lost somewhere, it might be because fairies are making you go the wrong way. Take off your coat, turn it inside out and put it on again. This will break the spell.

If you find yourself face to face with
a dangerous fairy, remember that they are
terribly sensitive and prickly. If you make
them angry, they might pounce on you,
shoot enchanted arrows into you –
or even snatch you away! So:

★ Don't be cheeky.

★ Don't tell any lies or make any promises.

★ Don't be greedy, mean, or refuse to do the fairy a favour.

★ Above all, never take even the tiniest taste of food or
drink from a fairy, no matter how delicious it looks.
It will almost certainly be tainted with magic.
As soon as you taste it,
the fairies will be able
to take you prisoner
and keep you hidden
away for ever!

Changelings

Sometimes bad fairies kidnap babies or even big children. They usually leave a 'changeling' – a fairy child – in the real child's place.

At first, the changeling looks like the real child, but underneath it is very different. As time passes, it becomes either hideously ugly or breathtakingly beautiful.

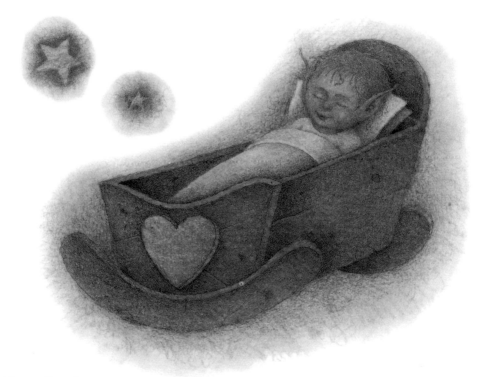

Changelings have strange powers.

They can see in the dark. They can play music so exquisitely that they bring tears to listeners' eyes. But they are often fierce, bad-tempered and vicious. They cry and scream. They bite, scratch and kick – and no one can stop them.

How to Swop a Changeling

★ Make it laugh (that's not so easy: fairies don't usually find anything funny!)

★ Ask the changeling to tell you how old it is. If you can persuade it to admit that it's 100 or even 1,000 years old, you will have broken the spell.

★ Spoil it! Give it lots of delicious food. Overwhelm it with wonderful gifts and treats. Its fairy mother will be so grateful to you, she will take it away and give back the real child.

The Boy who was Stolen by Fairies

A boy was once stolen by fairies. They treated him kindly, and taught him how to dance and make beautiful silver swords.

But the boy's parents were terribly upset, for the changeling left in the boy's place was thin and yellow, with a pinched face like an old man.

They went to a wise man for advice. He told them to throw the changeling into the fire. As soon as they did, the changeling flew up to the ceiling, burst a great hole in it and disappeared through the roof into the night!

Next, the wise man sent the boy's father out into the hills at midnight, carrying a sleeping cockerel in his arms. The father soon found the fairies out there dancing – and there was his son right in the middle of them. "Give me back my boy!" he yelled, but the fairies just laughed.

The sound of their laughing woke the cockerel, and it crowed loudly. At once the fairies froze with fear. They threw the boy back to his father, disappeared into the hill and never caused any trouble again.

Are Fairies Real?

Some people say that even if fairies really existed once, they have long gone, died out and disappeared.

They say that there's no room for fairies in the modern world. They say that all the fairies must surely have been crushed by machines, broken by busy roads and pushed out by the spread of dirty, bustling cities. These people will assure you that you'll never see a real fairy anywhere today.

But maybe these people are wrong. Maybe the fairies are simply hiding away. Maybe some are still here with us, sleeping or watching us from secret places where we've never thought of looking. Some of these fairies may still be very close.

Into the Mountains

A boy and a girl in the Scottish Highlands once saw a long procession of fairy people riding past and disappearing into a tunnel in the mountains.

"We're going home for ever," the fairies called out to them. "You'll never see the likes of us in your world again!"

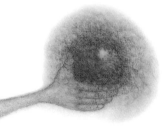

If you search carefully, you may still find signs of fairies:

A mound in the grass
may be covering up a secret entrance
to Fairyland.

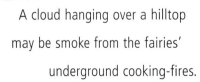

A cloud hanging over a hilltop
may be smoke from the fairies'
underground cooking-fires.

A ring of toadstools
in the grass may mark
a spot where the fairies
came out to dance in the night.

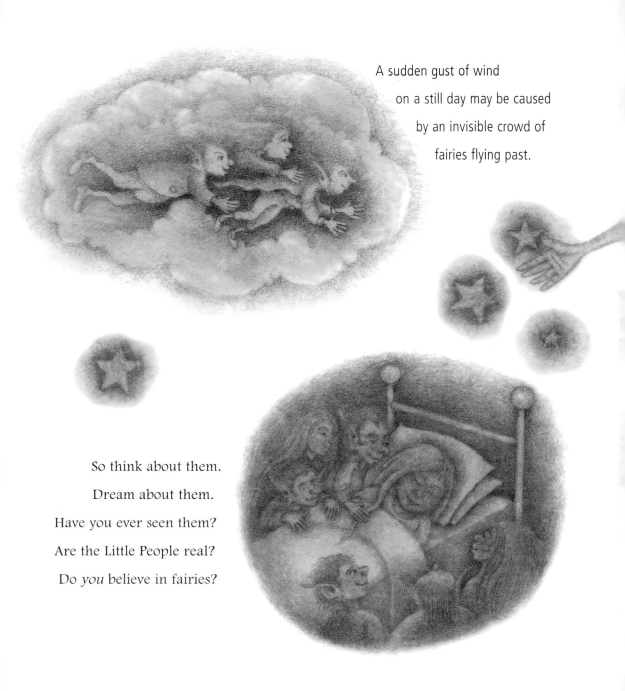

A sudden gust of wind
on a still day may be caused
by an invisible crowd of
fairies flying past.

So think about them.
Dream about them.
Have you ever seen them?
Are the Little People real?
Do *you* believe in fairies?

Fairy Sources

The information and stories in this book are based on authentic folklore and folk tales. Until the early 20th century, belief in fairies was still widespread amongst country people throughout Britain, Ireland and many other European countries.

N. Arrowsmith with G. Moorse: A Field Guide to the Little People *London: Macmillan 1977*

L. T. Blecher & G. Blecher: Swedish Folktales and Legends *New York: Pantheon Books 1993*

K. M. Briggs: The Fairies in Tradition and Literature *London: Routledge & Kegan Paul 1967*

K. M. Briggs: The Vanishing People: A study of Traditional Fairy Beliefs *London: Batsford 1978*

K. M. Briggs: Dictionary of British Folktales *London: Routledge & Kegan Paul 1971*

K. M. Briggs: British Folktales and Legends: A Sampler *London: Paladin 1977*

J. Jacobs: Celtic Fairy Tales *London: David Nutt 1892*

J. Jacobs: English Fairy Tales *London: the Bodley Head 1968*

G. Jarvie (Ed).: Irish Folk and Fairy Tales *London: Penguin 1992*

G. Jarvie (Ed.): Scottish Folk and Fairy Tales *London : Penguin 1992*

T. Keightley: The Fairy Mythology *London: G. Bell 1878*

M. Leach (Ed.): Funk & Wagnall's Standard Dictionary of Folklore, Mythology and Legend *New York: Harper & Row 1984*

R. Mannheim (trans.): The Penguin Complete Grimms Tales for Young and Old *London: Penguin 1984*

N. & W. Montgomerie: The Well at the World's End *London: The Hogarth Press 1956*

E. Quayle: The Magic Ointment and other Cornish Legends *London: Andersen Press 1986*

E. Sheppard-Jones: Welsh Legendary Tales *London: Thomas Nelson & Sons 1959*

C. White: A History of Irish Fairies *Dublin: The Mercier Press 1976*